Clifford
The Big Red Dog

For the real Emily Elizabeth

This special edition was printed in 2011 for Kohl's Department Stores, Inc.
(for distribution on behalf of Kohl's Cares, LLC, its wholly owned subsidiary) by Scholastic Inc.

Kohl's
0-545-22897-2
123386
04/11

ISBN 978-0-545-22897-8

10 9 8 7 6 5 4 3 2 1   11 12 13 14 15 16/0

Printed in China   127
This edition printing, May 2011

Clifford
The Big Red Dog

Norman Bridwell

SCHOLASTIC INC.

New York   Toronto   London   Auckland

Sydney   Mexico City   New Delhi   Hong Kong

I'm Emily Elizabeth,

and I have a dog.

My dog is a big red dog.

Other kids I know have dogs, too.

Some are big dogs.

And some are red dogs.

But I have the biggest, reddest dog on our street.

This is my dog—Clifford.

We have fun together. We play games.

I throw a stick, and he
brings it back to me.

He makes mistakes sometimes.

We play hide-and-seek.

I'm a good hide-and-seek player.

I can find Clifford,

no matter where he hides.

We play camping out,

and I don't need a tent.

He can do tricks, too.

He can sit up and beg.

Oh, I know he's not perfect.

He has *some* bad habits.

He runs after cars.

He catches some of them.

He runs after cats, too.

We don't go to the zoo anymore.

He digs up flowers.

Clifford loves to chew shoes.

It's not easy to keep Clifford.

He eats and drinks a lot.

His house was a problem, too.

But he's a very good watchdog.

The bad boys don't come around anymore.

One day I gave Clifford a bath.

And I combed his hair,

and took him to the dog show.

I'd like to say Clifford won first prize.

But he didn't.

I don't care.

You can keep all your small dogs.

You can keep all your black,

white, brown, and spotted dogs.

I'll keep Clifford . . . . Wouldn't you?

Clifford's
Family

To Shane Stalling

Clifford's
Family

Norman Bridwell

SCHOLASTIC INC.

New York   Toronto   London   Auckland
Sydney   Mexico City   New Delhi   Hong Kong

I'm Emily Elizabeth, and this is my dog.

His name is Clifford.

We live in a small town now, but we were both born in the city.

One day we went back to visit
our old home in the city.

CITY
10 MI

Clifford hadn't seen his mother since he was a tiny puppy.

She hardly knew him.

She still treated him like a puppy.
She checked his teeth.

And she looked at his ears to see if he
had been washing them.

The man told us where Clifford's brother and sisters lived. We went to find them.

Clifford's sister, Claudia, lived nearby.
She was taking her owner for a walk.

We went to the park with them. A taxi was blocking the crosswalk.

Clifford took care of that.

Next we found his brother, Nero.

Nero was a rescue dog at a fire station.

While we were there, the alarm rang. We followed the fire truck. Nero rushed into the building.

Clifford helped him.

Nero was very brave.

Then we set off to the country. Clifford's other sister, Bonnie, was a farm dog.

One of Bonnie's jobs was to herd sheep into their pen.

Clifford wanted to do some farm work too.

He started to drive the cows toward the barn.

One of the cows was a bull, and
bulls don't like the color red.

Clifford wasn't scared—he was smart.
He didn't want to hurt the bull,
so he jumped out of the way.
When Clifford jumps, he really jumps!

We had one more place to visit. It was
Clifford's father's home in a town nearby.

The house was small, and there were
a lot of kids playing in the yard.

Clifford's father didn't have a collar, or a dog dish, or a doghouse. But he seemed very happy.

I guess it was the kids. He sure loved kids.
He was a lot like Clifford, just a little smaller.

Clifford wished his family could
come and live with us.
But they all had people
who needed them...

...just as I need Clifford,
the best dog of all.